Peak Dale Farm Stories

Valentine's Day

For Alice and Joseph – B.D.
For Penny and Bryan – K.L.

CATNIP BOOKS
Published by Catnip Publishing Ltd
14 Greville Street
London EC1N 8SB

First published 2009
1 3 5 7 9 10 8 6 4 2

A CIP catalogue record for this book is available from the British Library.

ISBN 978 1 846470 89 9

Printed in Poland

www.catnippublishing.co.uk

Peak Dale Farm Stories

Valentine's Day

Berlie Doherty

Illustrated by Kim Lewis

Catnip

Contents

A calf who thinks he's a sheep

Anna lives on a farm near an old stone bridge, with a river winding past. There are sheep on the hills and cows in the field. There are chickens in the barns and in the croft behind the house. There's a pony in the orchard and his name is Silver.

There's an old red tractor in the yard. The farmer is called William. His wife is called Jean and she's warm and kind. They're Grandpa Bill and Nanny Jean. And there's Uncle Dusty with hair like a cloud. They all live together in Peak Dale Farm.

Anna's living there till her mother gets better. She's in a hospital far away in London.

Every morning, Anna and Nanny Jean collect the eggs from the hen shed in the croft. They find twelve eggs, and then Anna slides her hand under a hen called Comfy. She finds her very own breakfast egg there, warm in her hand. Then before she goes to school, and as soon as she comes home, she goes to feed Valentine.

Valentine is a white calf. He isn't very well-behaved. He used to live in the croft with the hens, till he trod on all the eggs. He was moved to the camping field, till he went into one of the tents and pulled it down on top of him.

Uncle Dusty wanted to sell him, but he agreed that if Valentine behaved himself, he could stay on the farm till Anna goes home.

"We'll put him in a big field with the sheep and cows," he said. "And we'll see if he knows how to be good."

"He does," said Nanny Jean, and she and Anna smiled at each other.

At first, Valentine behaved himself very well in the big field. He didn't much like the cows, and they didn't much like him, but he

made friends with the sheep and the lambs. He really thought he was one of them, even though he was bigger than even the biggest sheep by now. When Cassie the sheepdog tried to round them up, he ran with them this way and that across the field.

"He still thinks he's a sheep," Anna laughed.

"He's happy," Nanny said. "He'll behave like a calf one day, you'll see."

Valentine in trouble

Anna goes to the little village school, just over the hill from Peak Dale Farm. At first she was worried about going, but she soon made a friend there. He was called Chris, and he was the only one in the school who was the same age as Anna. He lived in the last cottage in the valley, just up the hill from Peak Dale Farm. They were always the last to get off the bus, and sometimes Chris would come to the gate of the big field with Anna. She would call "Valentine!" and the calf would trot over to her and butt her head and tread on her toes and lick her ear. Chris would stroke him, and then he would run off to his cottage up the hill, and Anna would run to the kitchen of Peak Dale Farm to see Nanny Jean.

One day Chris and Anna were bumping along on the bus, when the driver pulled up sharply.

"By 'eck!" he shouted. "What's going on?"

He swerved the bus into a passing-place, and the children stared out of the window as a parade of animals wandered past. Two ewes, five lambs, three Jersey cows – and they were led by a small white calf.

"Let me out!" shouted Anna. "That's Valentine!"

"No way," the driver shouted back. "It's my job to see you home, and see you home I will, young lady!"

As soon as they reached the farm, Anna and Chris jumped off the bus. Anna could see the red tractor up the hill. "Grandpa Bill! Grandpa Bill!" she shouted, but he was too far away to hear. She could see Uncle Dusty on his new blue quad bike, but he was having a great time roaring up and down the field and he couldn't hear her either. She ran into the kitchen, where Nanny Jean was making fruit scones for tea.

"Valentine's broken through a hedge," she shouted, hopping up and down with excitement. "And all the animals are walking down the lane."

Nanny Jean rubbed her floury hands on her skirt and came running out of the kitchen. Chris and Anna ran ahead of her towards the lane.

"Don't chase them!" Nanny

Jean warned. "Once they start running we'll never catch them. If they get as far as the main road, there'll be an accident." She opened the wicket gate into a side field. "Come this way, and we might get to the big road before they do, and head them back into a field. I'll get Cassie. You two run as fast as you can!"

Chris could run very fast. Anna could run quite fast. Nanny Jean could run a bit, stop, have a breather, and run again. But

Cassie the sheepdog could run like the wind.

All four of them ran across the side field, over the stile to the big field, through a gate to the next field, and out right across it to the far gate at the corner, near the road junction. Cassie seemed to know exactly what she was doing. By the time Chris arrived she was already under the last gate and into the lane. By the time Anna arrived, Cassie was already crouching down, facing the procession of animals. Valentine came to a surprised stop, and all the other animals bumped into him. They stood stock still in front of Cassie.

At last Nanny Jean arrived. "Well done everyone!"

She opened the gate wide, whistled sharply, and Cassie ran along the side of Valentine's procession and herded them through the gate and into the field. Nanny shut the gate just as a Land Rover came hurtling round the bend.

"My gosh!" she panted. "I haven't had such fun for a long time! Let's all go home and finish off those scones, shall we? And we can have them for tea."

And they did.

A job for Anna

Anna had been at Peak Dale farm for four months now. She wasn't afraid of the cows any more, or of Silver the horse, or the hens in the yard. She liked school, and she had lots of friends there, especially Chris. She loved being with Grandpa Bill and Nanny

Jean. Even Uncle Dusty made her smile sometimes. Most of all, she loved Valentine. He still trod on her toes and nibbled her ears. She went to see him every day, before school and after school, and when the holidays came she liked to sit in his field and draw pictures of him with his friends the sheep.

But she missed her mum very much. She wanted to see her again more than anything else in the world.

"Can I go home yet?" she asked

Nanny Jean, and her grandmother hugged her.

"Mummy's still very, very poorly," she said. "You won't be able to go home yet. And anyway, I need your help for the Hope Show." She filled the sink with dishes and dangled a tea towel in front of Anna.

"What's the Hope Show?"

"Well, all the farmers bring their best animals to Hope on Show Day, and show them to the judge to see which is best in its class. It's a competition. I'm going to be very busy showing Silver in the horse class. Grandpa Bill is going to be showing Titan."

Anna shuddered. Titan was a huge bull that was kept in his own field at the far end of the farm. She'd only seen him once, and he was enormous. She was definitely still scared of him. She dried the plates and piled them carefully on the table, trying not to think about Titan.

"Uncle Dusty will be taking

Cassie and some sheep to the Show for the sheepdog trials." Nanny Jean went on. They could hear sheep now in the yard, bleating and baa-ing as they were being herded into a transporter. "He has to let the judge see how clever Cassie is at rounding up sheep."

"Oh, she'll win! She'll win!" Anna said. She looked through the kitchen window at the yard. Uncle Dusty and Grandpa Bill were whooping and whistling as the sheep skittered in all the wrong directions. Cassie flattened herself to the ground and the sheep stood still, waiting to be told what to do next.

"I hope so. Uncle Dusty's trained her since she was a few months old, and she's the best dog we've ever had."

"Can I come and watch?"

"You'll be there, Anna. I've got a job for you." Nanny Jean lowered her voice. "We'd like to show something in the calf class, but we're all so busy. And then I thought, who can I ask? Why, Anna of course!"

"Me?" Anna looked worried.

"You and Valentine, Anna."

"Me and Valentine?" That didn't sound too bad. "But what do I have to do?"

"Not much. You'll be his handler. That means you'll have to look after him and make him look smart. You have to clean him the night before. I'll help you. You have to keep him clean on the day. That's not so easy! Then, when it's your turn, you have to put on a white coat so you'll look smart too. Then you just have to walk round the show field with him so the judge can have a good look at him and see how beautiful he is."

Anna was already worried. She twisted the tea towel in her hands anxiously. "Will there be any people there?"

Nanny Jean smiled. "A couple of thousand, I should think."

"A couple of thousand!"

"But you won't notice them.

You'll be too busy looking after Valentine."

"Please, please, Nanny Jean, don't ask me to do it," Anna wailed. "I can't. I can't!"

"Not even for me?" Nanny Jean asked.

"Ask Chris. He'll do it."

"Chris will be helping his dad on the wood-carving stall. He'll be busy all day. And anyway Anna, you wouldn't really want anyone else to show Valentine, would you?"

Anna knew she was right. She couldn't bear the thought of someone else leading Valentine round the show field. He'd be scared, without her. Scared of all those couple of thousand people.

"But Uncle Dusty doesn't even like Valentine," she said. "Doesn't he want one of the other calves to go to the show?"

"He wants it to be Valentine," Nanny Jean said. "You know Uncle Dusty wants to sell him, don't you?"

Anna nodded.

"If Valentine goes to the Show and lots of farmers see him there, Uncle Dusty would get a good price for him next market day."

"Then I definitely won't show him!" Anna said firmly.

"Ah, wait," Nanny Jean said. "He'll want to sell him anyway, Anna, sooner or later. But if Valentine does very well, Uncle Dusty might decide to keep him on the farm. Valentine might be as big as Titan one day, you see.

You never know. Anyway, we just have to make him look beautiful for the Show. That's the main thing."

Making Valentine look beautiful

The night before the Show, Anna and Nanny Jean got Valentine ready. They had to wash him with the hose-pipe, shampoo his hair, and hose him down again. He smelt wonderful. They combed him and brushed him as his hair dried. He skipped and frolicked and butted and nibbled, but somehow they managed to get him completely clean. Then they led him into a dry barn so he would stay clean all night.

"He really is beautiful!" Anna sighed. "Everyone will love him, even Uncle Dusty. Won't they?"

"Even Uncle Dusty," Nanny Jean agreed. "Unless he has a heart of wood. I sometimes think he has, you know."

Anna couldn't sleep that night. How on earth was she going to be able to walk round the field in front of two thousand people? It was impossible. She tossed and turned in her bed, and the thought of what she had to do became even more frightening. She cuddled her doll, Mrs Rattle, but it didn't help. Mrs Rattle didn't understand. At last Anna threw back her duvet and ran into her grandmother's room. Grandpa Bill was fast asleep and snoring noisily, but Nanny Jean was wide awake. She sat up when Anna ran in.

"I can't. I can't. I can't!" Anna sobbed.

"Come here Anna." Nanny Jean drew back the duvet so Anna could climb in to bed next to her. "You've been so brave since you came here. It was horrible for you when your mummy had the accident, and you had to come all this way and live with us. You'd never lived on a farm before. You were frightened of the hens and the cows and Silver, but we asked you to help and you did it. You

were worried about going to a new school, but you did it. And you've made friends there, haven't you? You were very frightened when you got lost in the woods that time, but it was all right in the end."

"Valentine helped," Anna sniffed.

"He certainly did. Now it's your turn to help him. Nobody else can do it. And I think that if you're brave enough to walk round that Show field tomorrow so everyone can see how beautiful Valentine is, you'll never be scared of anything again."

Nanny Jean stroked Anna's hair, and told her about all the things she used to be scared of when she was eight, like the creaky bridge that Anna ran over every day, and the wind hoo-ing down the chimney, and the sea when she saw it for the first time when she went on holiday to Scarborough.

"I thought it was alive," she said. "I didn't know what to make of it, and people were walking right into it! And I made myself step into it too. I think that was the bravest thing I ever did in my life!"

But Anna didn't say anything, because she was fast asleep.

The day of the Show

At six o'clock the next morning they all went together to inspect Valentine. Unbelievably, he was still clean.

"Righto," said Grandpa Bill. "He'll do. Let's get him in the trailer now."

Valentine hated the very idea of

this. He stood squarely in front of the trailer, bellowing at the top of his voice, and refused to go up the trailer ramp.

"Please Valentine. Please be good," Anna whispered in his ear, but he rolled his eyes and carried on bellowing. Nanny Jean pushed him, Grandpa Bill pulled him, and Uncle Dusty shouted at him, but it was no use.

"I knew Valentine would be trouble," Uncle Dusty grumbled. "Now we're all going to be late."

"Stop grumping, Dusty," Nanny Jean said. "He's scared, that's all."

"Don't be scared, Valentine," Anna said. Then she had a wonderful idea. "Maybe if you put some of his sheep friends in the trailer with him, he'll be happy."

Uncle Dusty snorted with annoyance, but luckily he had to take three sheep to the Show for the sheepdog trials. He bundled them into the trailer and Valentine trotted up the ramp after them, no trouble at all.

Anna shut the trailer gate and rubbed Valentine's ear.

"Good boy!" she said. "Now cheer up. This is Your Day!"

Uncle Dusty whistled to Cassie, who jumped up into the Land Rover with him, and they set off with Valentine and his three friends bumping along in the trailer behind him. Anna climbed into the other Land Rover with Nanny Jean. Silver was in the horse-box behind them.

"OK, Anna?" Nanny Jean asked.

Anna nodded and kept her eyes shut tight. I will do it, she told herself. It's Valentine's big day.

*

At the showground, Nanny Jean took Anna and Valentine to the green tent where the calves were being kept. Valentine was looking a bit dusty after the ride in the trailer, so they gave him another quick wash and dried him with a hair dryer.

"I'd better go and see to Silver now," Nanny Jean told Anna. "All you have to do is sit here with Valentine. Make sure he doesn't crawl under his rope and run away. I'll be back before you have to take him into the Show field." She gave Anna a kiss. "It's going to be a wonderful day, I promise."

Anna sat patiently by Valentine. At first he did his very best to roll under the rope, or to climb over it, but Anna stroked him and brushed him and told him what a wonderful day it was going to be, and that calmed him down. She could hear a buzz of voices outside the green tent. People were already arriving at the showground. A brass band started playing. Announcements were being made over a public address system, telling the visitors about all the attractions.

"Llamas, shire horses, bouncy castle, birds of prey, face-painting," the announcer said. "Sheepdog trials, horse, cattle and sheep shows. It's going to be a fantastic day ladies and gentlemen. Enjoy yourselves!"

Anna looked round at the other calves and decided that not one of them was as pretty as Valentine.

"Keep calm, keep calm," she told herself. "If I keep calm, he will too."

And she would have kept calm, in spite of the butterflies fizzing round her tummy, if she hadn't heard a sudden huge commotion from outside the tent. People were screaming, shouting, running about. The voice on the microphone begged everyone to stay calm.

"A bull has escaped from the Show field," the announcer said. "Stay calm. Please keep out of its way. Please bring children to the stage area."

Someone rushed into the green tent and ordered all the young handlers to leave at once in case the bull charged into it. Anna wanted to take Valentine with her but the steward grabbed her hand and rushed her out of the tent towards the big stage, which was raised above the ground. Anna

looked round anxiously. She couldn't see the bull, but she could see which way it was heading because of the way the crowds scattered away from it. She could see several men running after it, and right in front of them, the tallest of them all, was Uncle Dusty. Grandpa Bill was close behind him.

"Oh no!" Anna wailed. "It's Titan! Titan's escaped!"

Into the
Show field

Titan was caught at last. Uncle Dusty slipped a rope through his nose ring, and Grandpa Bill led him back to his trailer, ready to drive him home. The band started to play, the bouncy castle was re-opened, the ice-creams were back on sale, and the farm children were allowed back to their green tents.

Anna rushed straight to Valentine's pen. She couldn't believe what she saw. Valentine was rolling about on the ground, kicking his legs in the air. His coat was covered in grass, and his knees were bright green. How would she ever get him ready in time, all on her own? She scrambled under the rope and washed him down, scrubbed his knees, rubbed him down with a towel, brushed his coat. Then, just as she had managed to get him looking nice again, Nanny Jean arrived.

"Quick Anna! Get your white coat on. It's the calf show now!"

A thousand butterflies fluttered inside Anna's tummy. She could feel her heart bumping in her chest.

"Oh no!" she moaned. "Not yet! I'm not ready!"

Nanny slipped the white coat over Anna, tidied her hair, gave her the rope that fastened to

Valentine's halter, and led them both out of the tent towards the big Show field.

"What do I do?" Anna whispered. Her voice was shaking, and her hands were clammy with sweat.

"Just follow the others round the field. Listen and look. Watch the calf, watch the judge, and look happy! Now go!"

Anna didn't feel happy. She felt terrified. The big field was surrounded by hundreds of people. She wanted to run and hide.

Valentine did too. He tried to turn round, and she hung onto his lead and urged him on.

"Come on Valentine," she said. "It's you and me, together."

They walked slowly round the field. Out of the corner of her eye, Anna was aware of the judge and two other men standing in the middle of the field with clip-boards in their hands. Valentine stopped, and the calf behind them butted into him.

"Keep going, Anna!" she heard Nanny Jean shout.

"Good luck Anna," someone else said. She looked at the crowd, and saw Chris grinning at her. She smiled back and tugged gently at Valentine's lead. He moved forward and walked steadily by her side. It was getting a bit easier now. All the calves finished the circuit. Anna did as the other handlers did, stopped when they did, and stood beside Valentine. She felt calm and happy. She was enjoying herself. She looked at the judge and

smiled at him, and he smiled back and came towards her.

Anna started shaking again. The judge walked all the way round Valentine, looking carefully at him. Then he touched Valentine's side, and went to look at the other calves in the row. He touched two more. Their handlers led the calves into the centre of the field, Anna did the same. They stood right in the middle, with all those people watching, and Anna and Valentine kept completely calm. And then, to Anna's utter amazement, the judge touched Valentine again. One of the other men walked up and put a red rosette on Valentine's halter. Anna and Valentine kept perfectly still.

There was a squeal of excitement from the crowd. "Valentine! You did it! You won!" Nanny Jean shouted.

Anna's day

But that wasn't the end of the excitement. The judge went back to the other two men and looked at some notes. Then he cleared his throat to make an announcement.

"The award for the best young handler goes to – Anna May of Peak Dale Farm."

Anna couldn't believe it. She stepped forward and the judge bent down and shook her hand and gave her a rosette to pin to her white coat. She could feel her face glowing as red as the rosette. She wanted to dance with excitement, but she turned calmly and took Valentine's lead again. She could see the crowd now. She could see Nanny Jean waving and clapping. All the other prize winning animals were coming into the Show field for the grand parade.

The band began to play. The prize winners' names were called out, and again Anna had to step forward into the middle of the field. The judge gave her a shining silver cup. You would think that nothing better could happen that day, but it did.

As Anna walked with the other animals and their handlers round the field, past all the cheering crowds, she could see someone next to Nanny Jean. Someone pale and thin, sitting in a wheelchair.

Someone lifting her hand weakly to wave at her.

"Mummy!" Anna mouthed. She was so amazed and excited, she could hardly breathe. She wanted to leap over the rope fence and run to her mother and fling her arms round her in case she disappeared again. But she knew she mustn't. She mustn't leave Valentine's side. She was the best young handler, and Valentine was the best calf.

So she led Valentine round the

field, slowly and proudly. She went past all the cheering crowds. She went past Chris and her school friends, and Uncle Dusty and Grandpa Bill. And last of all, she went past Nanny Jean and Mum. Her smile was so big that she felt as if her face might burst.

When she came out of the Show field she led Valentine to the trailer. Uncle Dusty was waiting there for her. He shook hands with her, pumping her fist up and down.

"Grand, young 'un! By gum,

lass. You did grand!" he kept saying. "And so did our Valentine! Go and find your mum now, eh?"

Nanny Jean was pushing Mum's wheelchair towards her across the grass. Anna ran to her and stopped. She was nervous to touch her, she looked so thin and frail, but Mum leaned forward in her chair and pulled Anna towards her, and hugged her tight.

"My brave Anna!" Mum said. "I knew you could do it! I knew it!"

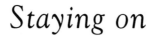

Staying on

Nanny Jean drove them back to the farm for a huge celebration tea. Anna's silver cup stood in the middle of the table. Uncle Dusty and Cassie had won a second prize rosette in the sheepdog trials. Nanny Jean and Silver had come third. Titan had disgraced himself by running away, and had been disqualified.

"He was still the grandest bull there," Uncle Dusty insisted. "He'd have won if he hadn't scarpered. But never mind." He winked at Anna. "In a few years' time Valentine will be as big and strong as him."

"Does that mean you're going to keep him, Uncle Dusty?" Anna asked.

Uncle Dusty slapped his hand on the table, making the plates jump. "It does! He'll be the prize bull one day, I can see that. We'll have to change his name though. Can't be going to the Hope Show with a bull called Valentine!"

They all laughed. Mum put out her hand and held Anna's in hers. "It's been a wonderful day. The best day for months!" she said.

"Are you really, really better?" Anna asked.

"Nearly, nearly better," Mum laughed. "I've still got a long way to go. But I'm getting there!"

"So can we go home?"

Mum shook her head. "Not yet Anna. I'm not that well yet. I still can't walk, and I've got to go back to hospital tomorrow. They let me out to see you today, because it's such a special day. And it's done me the world of good. But if you want to leave the farm we could move you to your other grandmother's, if you like, in London."

"We'd like you to stay a bit longer at Peak Dale Farm, Anna. But only if that's what you want.

What do you think?" Nanny Jean asked.

Anna looked round at them all. Uncle Dusty was anxiously scratching his cloud of grey hair. Grandpa Bill was tapping his fingers on the table, worried. Nanny Jean was half-smiling, half-frowning. Anna thought of her room up in the attic, where she could lie in bed at night and hear the river chitter-chattering over the stones and the owl calling his shivery hoo-hoo from the hollow tree. She thought of Comfy and the other hens in the croft, and the sheep and the cows in the field. She thought of mighty Titan and gentle Silver. She thought of Valentine, the best calf in the Show. The best calf in the world.

"Yes please," she said. "I want to stay."